THE BEAN FAMILY SPROUTS

GROWING STRONGER THROUGH NEW EXPERIENCES

D1096600

BY LORA SHAHINE, MD

ILLUSTRATED BY SARI JACK

The Bean Family Sprouts: Growing Stronger Through New Experiences

Thank you to Lucy Elenbaas for copy editing and publishing help.

ISBN: 978-0-9987146-6-0

No part of this book may be reproduced or distributed in any way without permission from the author. The information in this book is for educational purposes only and is not intended as medical advice or as a substitute for the advice of your healthcare professional.

Copyright © 2019 Lora Shahine. All Rights Reserved.

DEDICATED TO SARAH AND MILES

Congratulations on the new experiences you've conquered so far, and best wishes on those in your future!

From my Family to yours!

Meet the Bean Family.

The Bean Family was a happy one.

Living, eating, and playing in the dirt.

Baby Bean was so happy in his dirt home.
He couldn't imagine anything better.

But one day...

Baby Bean started to sprout.

He had little sprouts growing out of his body!

Baby Bean ran to his parents. He was shocked to see them sprouting too!
But they seemed happy...

Mrs. Bean told Baby Bean, "We're sprouting, Baby Bean!
We're getting ready to grow. Soon we will turn into plants and see the world!"

Baby Bean was sad. Baby Bean was scared!

Baby Bean liked his dirt home. He liked his dirt dinner
and the way things were.

Baby Bean could feel his sprouts getting bigger. He could feel them pushing up against the surface. He tried his best to stay in the dirt, but...

Try as he might, Baby Bean could not stay in that dirt.
He sprouted through the ground, and...

He saw things he'd never seen before.

He saw beautiful things, like the sun. He saw flowers, trees, and birds.

Baby Bean was so very happy.

The Bean Family was so very happy.

Baby Bean missed his dirt home. But he was excited about his new home and all the new things to do and see above ground.

Baby Bean realized that although change was hard, it was also an opportunity to be brave and experience new and exciting things!

DEAR READER,

I hope you've enjoyed this story and the beautiful illustrations about Baby Bean learning how to navigate his transition from a comfortable life underground to a brand new world above ground. Change is difficult, and any new experience brings emotions – from excitement and exhilaration to nervousness and fear. As a mother, I watch my children struggle with new schools, new teachers, new friends, new camps. Each new experience has brought a new worry and challenged them to be brave and try. It takes courage to try something new.

I have noticed through the years that with each new situation, my children look back on previous transitions as a means to build resilience. A new school year now is not as tough as the very first new school year. As a family, we can reflect on how nervous we were the first time we tried a new instrument, had a new teacher, or made a new friend and remember positive things about each new situation. We build on our past experiences.

My hope is that with this book, families can reflect on their new experiences and the emotions they bring. Children can connect with how scared and nervous Baby Bean is as he watches his body change, his life underground change, but also watch him enjoy his new life above ground. Without change, Baby Bean would not be able to enjoy his new surroundings and see all the beauty around the world above the ground. We cannot grow, thrive, and build resilience without change. It does not mean it's easy, but we can take it one step at a time and reflect on all we've learned from the experience together.

ENJOY!

Lora Shahine, MD

TIPS ON SUPPORTING YOUR CHILD THROUGH A NEW EXPERIENCE

Be patient, supportive, and encouraging in a positive way.

Focus on success as a willingness to try a new experience – to participate in the music lesson, not necessarily to be able to play a new piece on the piano at the end of the first lesson.

Make a 'Brave Diary' or 'Courageous Journal' where you write down times your child has been brave or courageous and bring it out when they need a little reminder. You can take pictures and put them up in their room or in the family room as reminders.

Act out new experiences and think through what could happen. New school year? Practice 'meeting' the new teacher at home and talk through the feelings that may come up.

Think of times you have been scared about trying something new but did it anyway and share that story with your child – even grown-ups get nervous with new experiences!

Focus less on the end goal but more on the process of learning, the small steps of being brave, and supporting your children along the way.

For more resources on how to help children with transitions and new experiences, try these resources:

American Academy of Pediatrics (AAP): aap.org

Healthy Children Parenting Website (by the AAP): healthychildren.org

LORA SHAHINE, MD Text and concept by Dr. Lora Shahine, physician, author, wife, friend, mother of two, and daughter to a life learner, librarian, and English teacher, Mrs. Charlene Ewing, who taught her family the importance of reading and the love of learning. Dr. Shahine, a reproductive endocrinologist born in North Carolina and educated for way too many years at Georgetown University, Wake Forest University School of Medicine, University of California at San Francisco, and Stanford University, practices infertility and miscarriage care at Pacific NW Fertility and the University of Washington in Seattle, WA. She is a mother who reaches for books for answers when life throws curve balls and writes books to help others navigate this journey called life. You can find more books, resources, and blog posts by Dr. Shahine on her website, *drlorashahine.com*, and follow her on most social media platforms @drlorashahine.

SARI JACK Illustrations by Sari Jack, an artist, illustrator, and designer whose work explores the beauty and mystery of nature and the environments we live in. She creates oil and watercolor paintings as well as graphic illustrations of all kinds. As a lifelong native to Seattle, WA, Sari draws great inspiration from her unique surroundings in the Pacific Northwest. She studied fine art and art history at Western Washington University and graphic design at Seattle Central Creative Academy. You can follow her work on her website, *sarijack.com*, and on social media @sari_jack.

Made in the USA
Columbia, SC
21 December 2019

85608410R00015